Dedicated to all the teachers
out there who embrace all of the
unique qualities of their students.

My name is Kale and I always think for myself.

Especially at school.

Most of the kids at school say their favorite class is gym class.

But I'm Kale and I actually like painting in art class better!

When we drew family pictures at school, most of the kids drew their family in front of their house.

But I'm Kale and I decided to do the picture of my family on a gigantic mountain-top instead!

On the school bus,
everyone likes to play *I Spy.*

I'm Kale and I love that game,
so I'm going to play too!

During snack time all the kids like to trade with each other!

I'm Kale and I always trade with Billy because his mom sends him juicy blueberries and those are my favorite!

During craft time, my friends like to make colorful snowmen out of clay.

I'm Kale and I love doing that too! I put a cape on my snowman and make believe that he can fly!

When the kids play soccer at
recess, they all race to score goals!

That's fun! But I'm Kale and I
like to be the goalie instead!

My friends love to read books about construction trucks and freight trains. I like those too!

But I'm Kale and I actually like reading about forest animals more!

At lunch time, a lot of the other kids bring ham sandwiches.

But I'm Kale and I always ask my mom to make her home-made strawberry rhubarb Jam sandwiches! I won't even trade those for juicy blueberries!

Sometimes the kids aren't quiet when Mrs. Grey is trying to teach us something.

But I'm Kale and I always try to pay attention when she's talking because I know how it feels when people don't listen to me.

In music class, we always play *Row, Row, Row Your Boat* on our recorders.

I'm Kale and I like to dance while we play the song! It's so much fun!

I'm Kale. I'm a clever and unique boy and I always think for myself!

Hello Readers!

I am an independent author and Amazon reviews can make a huge difference to the overall success for this book and of my Holistic Thinking Kids Series! If you enjoyed reading this book as much as I enjoyed writing it, please consider taking a few moments to leave a quick review. I would really appreciate it!

Thank you!

Kristy Hammill

CPSIA information can be obtained
at www.ICGtesting.com
Printed in the USA
LVHW071927100320
649600LV00002B/44